This book belongs to:

Logan and Matthew Kirste

Love Bubbie Harriet

Trip to Destin, Florida April 21, 2021

Apple Pie Publishing

Apple Pie Publishing, LLC
P.O. Box 1135
Rockwall, TX 75087
www.applepiepub.com

Editors Emily and Kathleen Feigen
Book Design by Michael Albee - michaelalbee.com

The text for this book is set in Optima, Century Gothic, Candy Script and Snickles. The illustrations in this book are rendered in colored pencil. Manufactured in the U.S.A. with lead free ink and paper.
10 9 8 7 6 5 4 3

Shapley-Box, Diane.
Tator's Swamp Fever / written and illustrated
by Diane Shapley-Box.
-- 1st ed. p. cm.

SUMMARY: Tator the Gator discovers the value of reading books while helping cure his sick mother in the swamplands.

Audience: Ages 2-7.
LCCN 2014939107
ISBN-13: 978-0-692-20847-2

Collect all the
Apple Bunch Books

QUALITY BOOKS MADE IN AMERICA

To my husband Kevin, sons Patrick & Mitchell

and to Mom & Dad

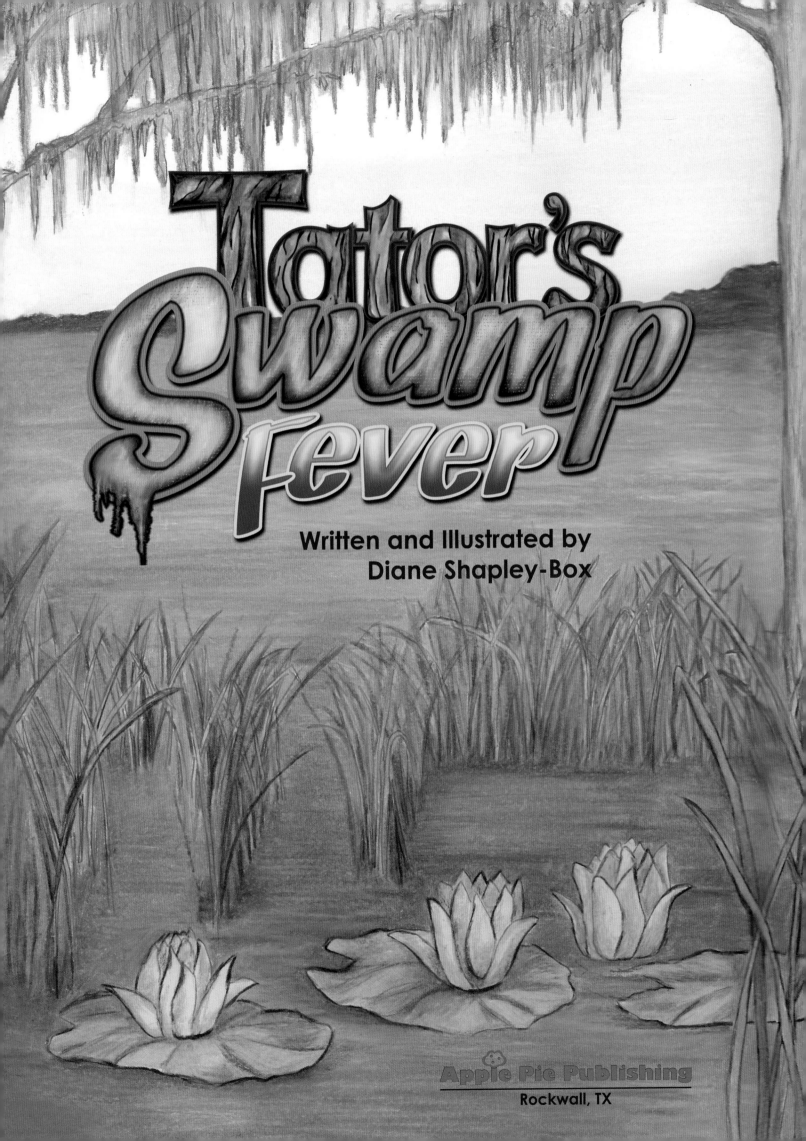

Tator's Swamp Fever

Written and Illustrated by
Diane Shapley-Box

Apple Pie Publishing
Rockwall, TX

Fred the Frog was excited as he ran up the street.

He thought, "Today is the day our book club will meet.

I have a new book I will share with my friends.

I will read the story and see how it ends."

Fred sat with his friends under a large apple tree.

He read about a turtle that swam in the sea.

Cabbit the Rabbit listened to Fred read his book.

Perdie the Birdie flew close to get a good look.

Fred would always ask Tator the Gator to go.

However, Fred's pal Tator would always say "No.

Reading books is not for me. I have no need at all.

Everything I need to know I learned when I was small."

t the book club meeting, they heard Tator cry, "Boo Hoo.
My mom is really sick with the alligator flu."
Cabbit looked at Perdie, and Perdie looked at Fred.
They ran to comfort Tator, though not a word was said.

Tator's friends gave him a hug, then jumped into his car.

Tator knew the way to go and knew it would be far.

They traveled to the swamplands where Tator's mom calls home.

They traveled to a place where the alligators roam.

They drove until the ground changed from dry to soggy.

In the swamp, they found Tator's mom tired, sad, and groggy.

Tator knelt by his mom and patted her on the cheek.

She tried to say hello, but her voice was just too weak.

Fred said, "We need a doctor to tell us what to do."

Cabbit pointed to a sign that read 'DOCTOR FIX-U.'

Perdie flew to the door, where she knocked BANG-BANG-BANG.

Out came a white alligator with one crooked fang.

*T*he rare alligator said, "Please come inside."
Entering his office, their eyes opened wide.

The friends had never seen so many books before.

Books were stacked to the ceiling and scattered on the floor.

The wise alligator knew Tator's mom was sick.

Her fever was too high and her ankles were too thick.

He blew dust off a book and handed it to Tator.

The title on the cover read, *CURES FOR A GATOR.*

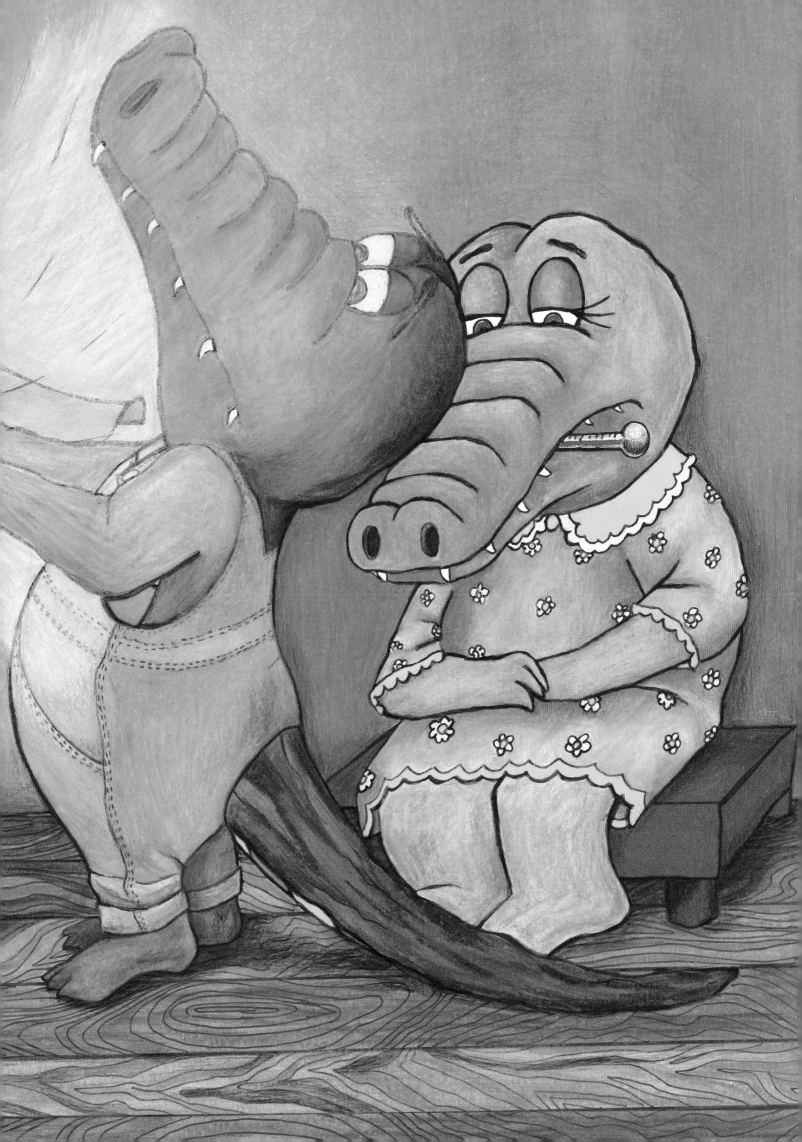

Fred flipped through the pages, and he read what to do.
"To help your mother," Fred said, "we must make a stew.
The ingredients we need are listed in this book.
The swampland is the place we will need to look."

A branch from a mangrove tree was first on the list.

Fred grabbed onto a branch then gave the limb a twist.

He noticed eyes gleaming in the murky swamp below.

Tator broke the branch off then said, "WE BETTER GO!"

Fred gathered clumps of moss that hung down from the trees.
Perdie snatched a snakeskin blowing in the breeze.
Cabbit found four floating flowers. She picked them one-by-one.
They had all the ingredients. Their search was finally done.

The friends returned to Tator's mom's little water shack.
Tator's mother was too sick to notice they were back.
Fred said, "We must start a fire and make it really hot.
We will put everything we found into a great, big pot."

The stew was finally ready in the afternoon.
Tator gave his mom a taste with a wooden spoon.

*T*ator's mom slept after she ate her special stew.

When she awoke, she said, "I feel as good as new.

Thank you all for helping me and for all that you have done.

Now, I can dance a gator dance with my gator son."

Now, Tator loves to meet with his book club friends.

He likes to read a book and find out how it ends.

Tator knows reading is important after all.

Books are fun to read whether you are big or small.

Swamp

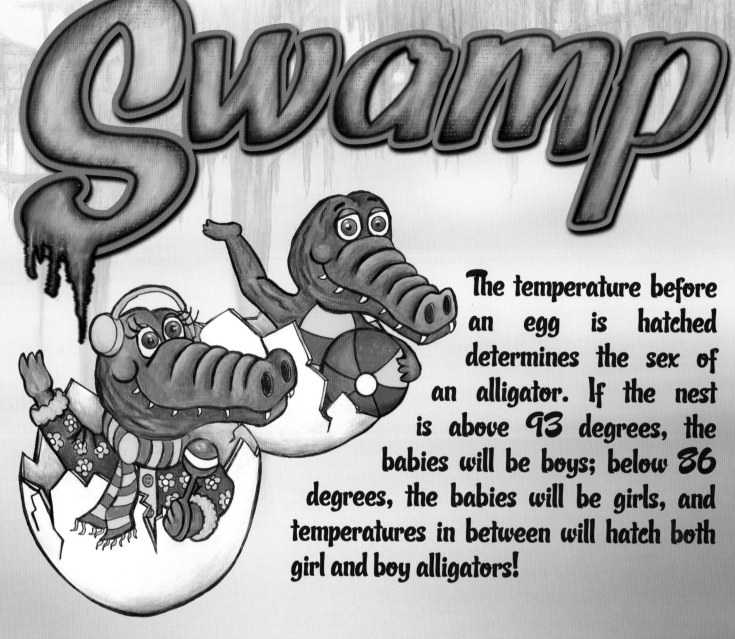

The temperature before an egg is hatched determines the sex of an alligator. If the nest is above 93 degrees, the babies will be boys; below 86 degrees, the babies will be girls, and temperatures in between will hatch both girl and boy alligators!

Years ago, it was common to use spanish moss to fill mattresses and couches.

Albino alligators cannot go out in the sun because their skin will burn.

An alligator can go through **2,000** to **3,000** teeth in a lifetime!

Egrets can sometimes be seen perched on top of alligators!

Snakes have no eyelids! They have a thin coat of skin/membrane that covers their eyes. Snakes shed their skin several times a year.

Fun Facts

Roscoe

Gizmo

Zorro

Sammie

Bella

Apples for Fred
Solving Problems

Tator's Big Race
Competition

Marvin

Rhett

Traveling across America . . .

The **Apple Bunch** buddies are not the only animals featured in the adventures of Fred, Tator, Perdie and Cabbit. See if you can find all the family pets – Zorro, Skip, Rhett, Marvin, Bella, Sarge, Achilles, Haylee, Roscoe, Gizmo and Sammie - that stop by throughout Diane Shapley-Box's award-winning series.

Achilles

Skip

Haylee

Sarge

Emerald Coast
Making New Friends

Swamp Fever
Learning New Things

Texas Stampede
Paying Attention

Christmas Star
Christmas Kindness

Collect all the Apple Bunch Books! **www.applepiepub.com**